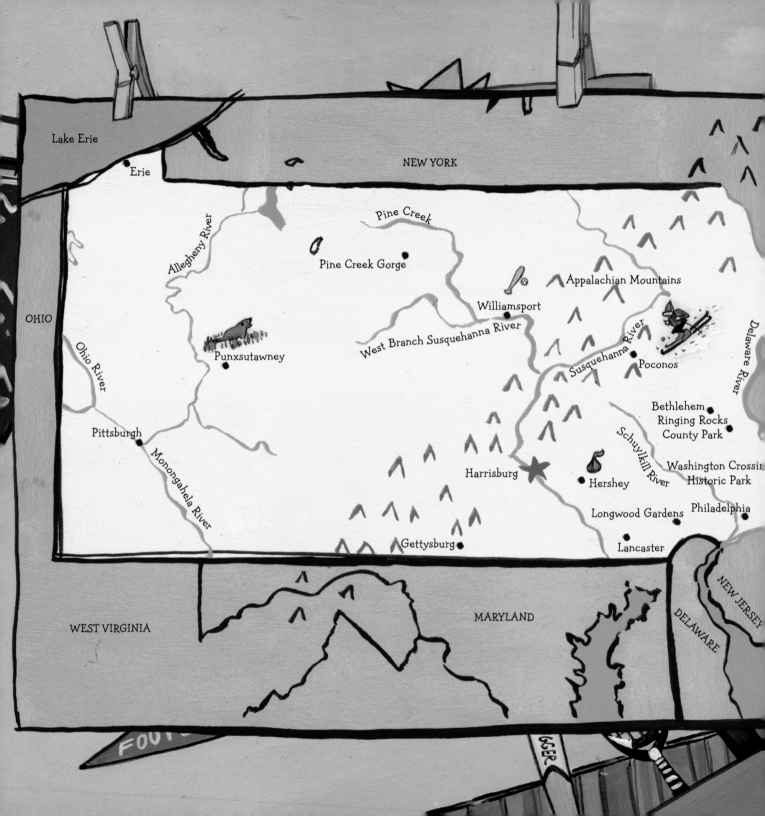

Lake Erie

Erie

NEW YORK

OHIO

Allegheny River

Pine Creek

Pine Creek Gorge

Appalachian Mountains

Williamsport

West Branch Susquehanna River

Susquehanna River

Punxsutawney

Poconos

Ohio River

Delaware River

Bethlehem
Ringing Rocks
County Park

Pittsburgh

Monongahela River

Schuylkill River

Washington Crossing
Historic Park

Harrisburg

Hershey

Philadelphia

Longwood Gardens

Lancaster

Gettysburg

WEST VIRGINIA

MARYLAND

NEW JERSEY

DELAWARE

FOOT

GGER

The Twelve Days of Christmas in Pennsylvania

written by
Martha Peaslee Levine

illustrated by
Rachel Dougherty

STERLING CHILDREN'S BOOKS
New York

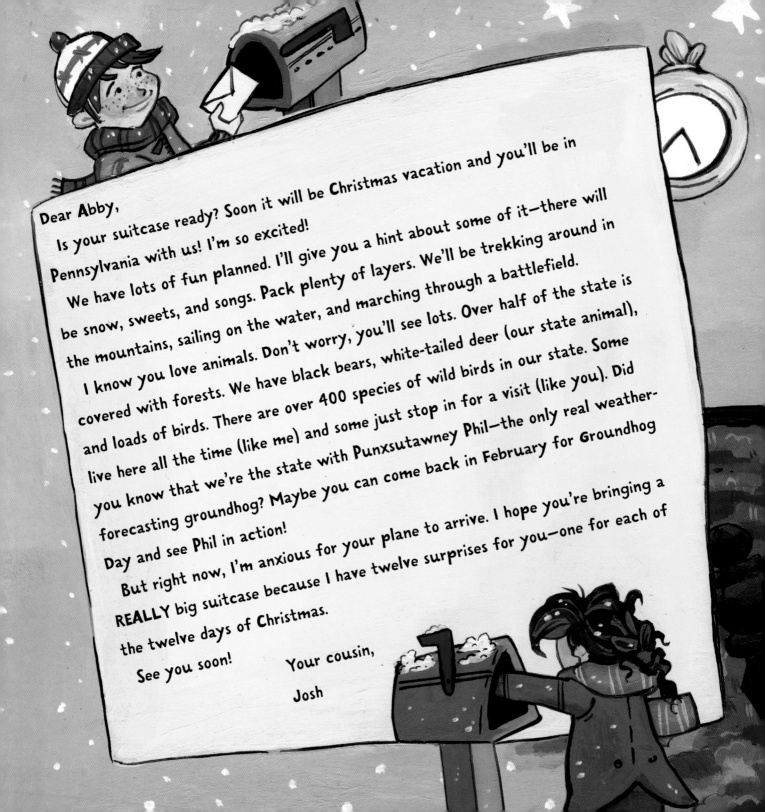

Dear Abby,

Is your suitcase ready? Soon it will be Christmas vacation and you'll be in Pennsylvania with us! I'm so excited!

We have lots of fun planned. I'll give you a hint about some of it—there will be snow, sweets, and songs. Pack plenty of layers. We'll be trekking around in the mountains, sailing on the water, and marching through a battlefield.

I know you love animals. Don't worry, you'll see lots. Over half of the state is covered with forests. We have black bears, white-tailed deer (our state animal), and loads of birds. There are over 400 species of wild birds in our state. Some live here all the time (like me) and some just stop in for a visit (like you). Did you know that we're the state with Punxsutawney Phil—the only real weather-forecasting groundhog? Maybe you can come back in February for Groundhog Day and see Phil in action!

But right now, I'm anxious for your plane to arrive. I hope you're bringing a REALLY big suitcase because I have twelve surprises for you—one for each of the twelve days of Christmas.

See you soon!

Your cousin,

Josh

Dear Mom and Dad,

I made it! Uncle Richard, Aunt Fay, and Josh were waiting for me at the airport in Philadelphia, and Josh already gave me my first present: my very own ruffed grouse! That's Pennsylvania's state bird. Some people call it a partridge—even John James Audubon, who painted all those amazing pictures of birds. I'm naming him Willy, after William Penn, who founded Pennsylvania. My little guy is Willy from Philly! He got so excited when he met me that he started drumming his wings. It sounded like Dad firing up his old lawnmower—the slow whir of the blades until finally the motor catches and kicks into gear.

Josh also gave me a little eastern hemlock, the state tree. Josh says when my tree is much older and produces cones, they'll end up looking like small bells . . . which is pretty perfect since our first stop after we left the airport was to see the famous Liberty Bell! Did you know the bell cracked the very <u>first</u> time it rang? Oops!

Next we walked over to Independence Hall—"the birthplace of the United States"! It was here that Benjamin Franklin, Thomas Jefferson, and others signed the Declaration of Independence. Uncle Richard bought us copies and Willy donated one of his beautiful tail feathers. We used it as a quill pen and signed our documents just like the Founding Fathers did way back in 1776.

Your Independent daughter,
Abby

On the first day of Christmas, my cousin gave to me . . .

a partridge in a hemlock tree.

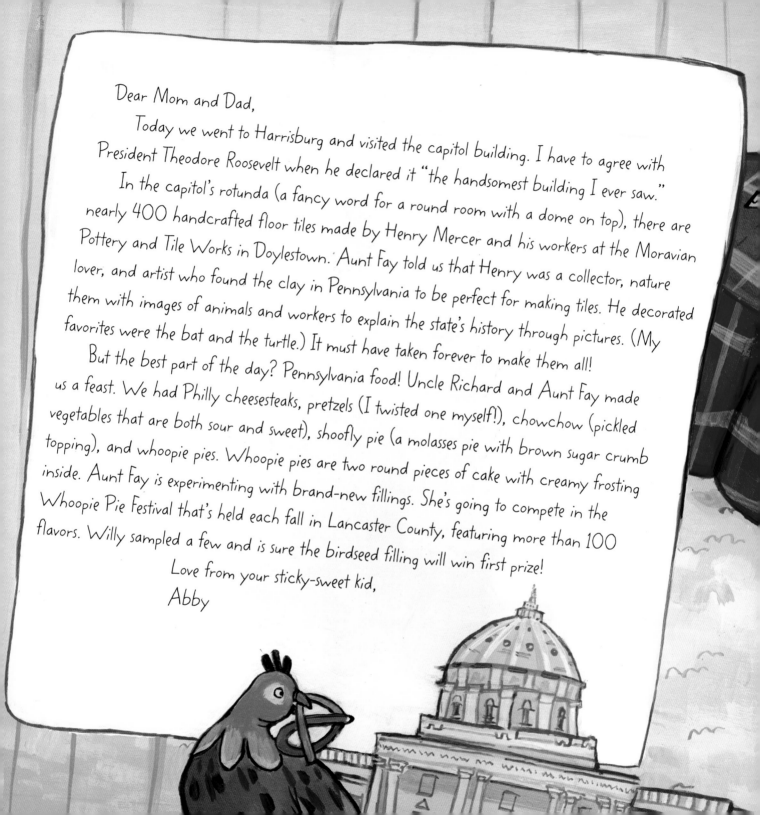

Dear Mom and Dad,

Today we went to Harrisburg and visited the capitol building. I have to agree with President Theodore Roosevelt when he declared it "the handsomest building I ever saw."

In the capitol's rotunda (a fancy word for a round room with a dome on top), there are nearly 400 handcrafted floor tiles made by Henry Mercer and his workers at the Moravian Pottery and Tile Works in Doylestown. Aunt Fay told us that Henry was a collector, nature lover, and artist who found the clay in Pennsylvania to be perfect for making tiles. He decorated them with images of animals and workers to explain the state's history through pictures. (My favorites were the bat and the turtle.) It must have taken forever to make them all!

But the best part of the day? Pennsylvania food! Uncle Richard and Aunt Fay made us a feast. We had Philly cheesesteaks, pretzels (I twisted one myself!), chowchow (pickled vegetables that are both sour and sweet), shoofly pie (a molasses pie with brown sugar crumb topping), and whoopie pies. Whoopie pies are two round pieces of cake with creamy frosting inside. Aunt Fay is experimenting with brand-new fillings. She's going to compete in the Whoopie Pie Festival that's held each fall in Lancaster County, featuring more than 100 flavors. Willy sampled a few and is sure the birdseed filling will win first prize!

Love from your sticky-sweet kid,
Abby

On the second day of Christmas, my cousin gave to me . . .

2 whoopie pies

and a partridge in a hemlock tree.

Dear Mom and Dad,

Did you know that in Hershey, Pennsylvania, the streetlamps are shaped like Hershey's Kisses? Milton Hershey set up his factory here to be near farmland and dairy cows. A LOT of milk goes into the 70 million Hershey's Kisses that are made here each and every day. The Kiss machines run twenty-four hours a day, seven days a week.

Josh's friend lives on a dairy farm near the Hershey's factory. I got to bottle-feed one of the calves! She gulped down the milk and then wiped her foamy mouth all over my jeans. She was so cute (but REALLY slobbery). The family shows their cows at the Pennsylvania Farm Show each year—it's the largest indoor farm event in the whole country. (I hope the calf I fed grows up to win a whole bunch of blue ribbons.)

As we warmed up inside the farmhouse with hot chocolate and fudge (made with fresh butter and cream, of course), Aunt Fay described the sheep-to-shawl contest at the Farm Show. A five-member team has only two and a half hours to shear a sheep, spin the wool, and weave the yarn into a shawl—that does NOT sound easy. Uncle Richard's favorite part of the show is the butter sculpture. Artists carve a statue out of <u>1,000 pounds</u> of butter!

Josh says there is often a HUGE snowstorm on Farm Show week. And snow means SNOW days off from school. Lucky Josh!

Love from your chocolate-dipped daughter,

Abby

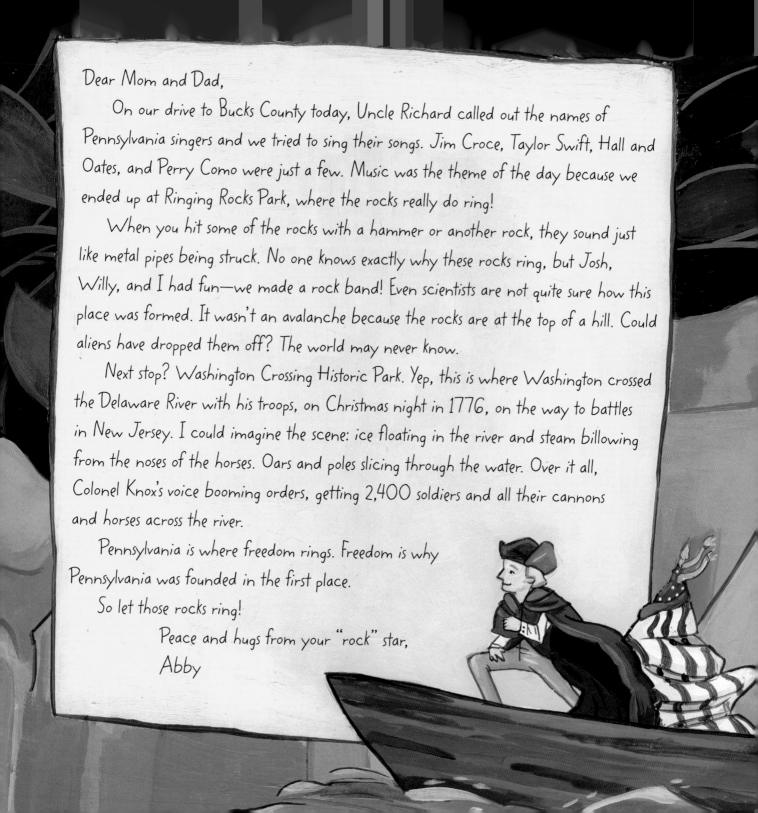

Dear Mom and Dad,

On our drive to Bucks County today, Uncle Richard called out the names of Pennsylvania singers and we tried to sing their songs. Jim Croce, Taylor Swift, Hall and Oates, and Perry Como were just a few. Music was the theme of the day because we ended up at Ringing Rocks Park, where the rocks really do ring!

When you hit some of the rocks with a hammer or another rock, they sound just like metal pipes being struck. No one knows exactly why these rocks ring, but Josh, Willy, and I had fun—we made a rock band! Even scientists are not quite sure how this place was formed. It wasn't an avalanche because the rocks are at the top of a hill. Could aliens have dropped them off? The world may never know.

Next stop? Washington Crossing Historic Park. Yep, this is where Washington crossed the Delaware River with his troops, on Christmas night in 1776, on the way to battles in New Jersey. I could imagine the scene: ice floating in the river and steam billowing from the noses of the horses. Oars and poles slicing through the water. Over it all, Colonel Knox's voice booming orders, getting 2,400 soldiers and all their cannons and horses across the river.

Pennsylvania is where freedom rings. Freedom is why Pennsylvania was founded in the first place.

So let those rocks ring!

Peace and hugs from your "rock" star,
Abby

On the fourth day of Christmas,
my cousin gave to me . . .

4 ringing rocks

3 milk cows, 2 whoopie pies,
and a partridge in a hemlock tree.

Hi, Mom and Dad,

Have you ever heard of a garden that's open even in the winter and has tree houses, carolers, half a million twinkling lights, and thousands of poinsettias? We visited a garden today that had ALL those things and more.

Longwood Gardens, near the town of Kennett Square, even has an organ with 10,010 pipes. The tallest pipe is 32 feet tall (that's as tall as a three-story building!) and the organ weighs 55 tons. With all that power, I think you can understand why I felt my insides jiggle when the organist played Christmas carols. Those low organ notes boomed out. It was like being right in the middle of an orchestra.

But my very favorite part of the gardens was the Secret Room. Can you guess what was in there? A Drooling Dragon! It's in the Children's Garden, which is full of stone animals and has seventeen fountains. Josh and I played hide-and-seek in the Bamboo Maze. We had fountains of fun!

Before we left, we built a snowman and helped decorate Christmas trees. Each one of us put a star on top—Willy included!

Love from your starry-eyed daughter,
Abby

On the fifth day of Christmas, my cousin gave to me . . .

5 golden stars

4 ringing rocks, 3 milk cows, 2 whoopie pies,
and a partridge in a hemlock tree.

Dear Mom and Dad,

Today we went to Lancaster County—Amish Country. The Amish people first began to come to Pennsylvania from Europe in the 1700s because they could celebrate their religion freely here.

They wear simple clothes to show their faith and don't use much modern technology—including electricity. That means no television and no computers! Their schools are one room. All the kids study together up to the eighth grade. After that, they work alongside their parents on the family farm and get educated "by doing."

To get around, the Amish use horses and buggies instead of cars. We went for a ride in a buggy. It was fun, but bumpy! We saw some families "raising a barn." Josh says that a barn can be built in <u>one</u> day because so many people show up to help. Amazing! The Amish call these events "frolics" because even though there is hard work to be done, these are special, fun occasions when everyone enjoys being together.

The Amish women make <u>beautiful</u> quilts. Aunt Fay has one hanging in her front hall. The stitches are so tiny. Good thing the women like sewing together, or it would take forever to finish!

Josh and Willy send their love and say "mach's gut!" That means "take care" in Pennsylvania German—the language that some descendants of German and Swiss immigrants here still speak.

Love from your bouncing and jouncing daughter,
Abby

On the sixth day of Christmas,
my cousin gave to me . . .

6 bumping buggies

5 golden stars, 4 ringing rocks, 3 milk cows, 2 whoopie pies,
and a partridge in a hemlock tree.

Dear Mom and Dad,

The Battle of Gettysburg was one of the main turning points in the Civil War (at least that's what Uncle Richard told me). Did you know this is where the Union stopped General Robert E. Lee's farthest invasion into the North? It's called the "High Water Mark of the Rebellion." The battle took place from July 1st to July 3rd, 1863, during the hottest time of the year. Even in that heat, the soldiers wore thick woolen uniforms. What's really sad is this was the bloodiest battle of the war. Millions of bullets were fired and more than 51,000 men became casualties, meaning they were killed, wounded, captured, or missing.

President Abraham Lincoln gave his famous Gettysburg Address right here—the speech that starts "Four score and seven years ago . . ." Do you know what four score is? A score is 20 years; so four score is 80 years! That's as old as Nana!

The most exciting part of the day? When the sun set, we saw ghosts! I'm totally not kidding. One was Abraham Lincoln. I could tell because of his tall top hat and beard. There were also soldiers toting guns and knapsacks. A large spirit dog dashed around their feet. Uncle Richard said there have been LOTS of ghost sightings in Gettysburg. I just never thought we'd be lucky enough to see some, too!

Spooky hugs,
Abby

On the seventh day of Christmas,
my cousin gave to me . . .

7 spooky spirits

6 bumping buggies, 5 golden stars,
4 ringing rocks, 3 milk cows, 2 whoopie pies,
. . . and a partridge in a hemlock tree.

Dear Mom and Dad,

Today in Pittsburgh, we rode the Monongahela Incline. It's the oldest continuously running funicular in the United States. (Isn't "funicular" a great word for a cable railway that travels up and down mountains? It has "fun" built right into its name!) There are only two inclines left in Pittsburgh, but there used to be seventeen. They carried people from their houses on Mount Washington, or "Coal Hill," down to the rest of the town around the river. The Germans who lived in Pittsburgh came up with the idea. They had cable cars like these back in Germany.

Then we went to the National Aviary, America's largest bird zoo. They have more than 500 birds from all around the world! Some of the 150 species are threatened or endangered in the wild. It's great that we could see them, and they were soooo colorful!

Willy found an old friend there—a snowy egret. The two of them organized a chorus of birds and trilled Christmas carols. Of course we had to join in. But the best part was when Josh taught me the "Chicken Dance." Even Uncle Richard shook his tail feathers!

Love from your bird-brained daughter,
Abby

On the eighth day of Christmas,
my cousin gave to me . . .

BIRDS

8 birds a-singing

7 spooky spirits, 6 bumping buggies,
5 golden stars, 4 ringing rocks,
3 milk cows, 2 whoopie pies,
and a partridge in a hemlock tree.

Ahoy! (That's sailor-speak for "hello, there!")

Did you know Lake Erie is the fourth largest of the Great Lakes but has the smallest amount of water? That made no sense to me until Aunt Fay explained that Lake Erie is really wide but not very deep.

We started the morning at the Erie Maritime Museum. The exhibits tell the story of Lake Erie beginning from the War of 1812. In that war, the United States battled the greatest naval power of the world—Great Britain. Commodore Oliver Hazard Perry commanded nine small ships, which defeated Great Britain's six much bigger ships. Perry and his men captured the entire British squadron, something that had never happened before.

The US Brig <u>Niagara</u> is a "tall ship" with two huge masts. It's one of the last remaining ships from the War of 1812. Although it had to be rebuilt in 1988, it looks just like the ship that Oliver Perry commanded. The <u>Niagara</u> stays docked at the Erie Maritime Museum when it is not off sailing the Great Lakes.

When we were there today, sailors were scrubbing down the decks—making everything shipshape (that means tidy). Willy even got in the act. He strapped two teeny brushes onto his feet and scrubbed away! One sailor pulled out a harmonica and blew Willy a tune.

"Fair winds and a following sea,"
Abby

On the ninth day of Christmas,
my cousin gave to me . . .

9 sailors swabbing

8 birds a-singing, 7 spooky spirits,
6 bumping buggies, 5 golden stars,
4 ringing rocks, 3 milk cows, 2 whoopie pies,
and a partridge in a hemlock tree.

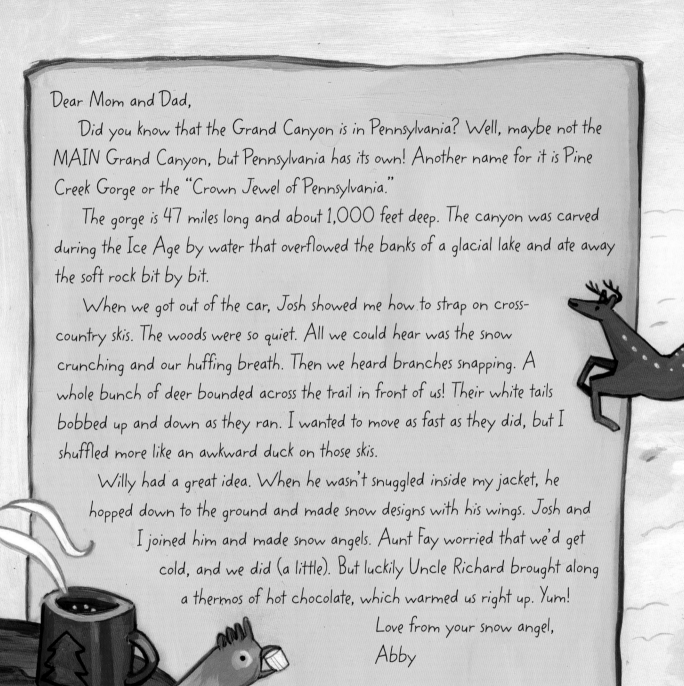

Dear Mom and Dad,

Did you know that the Grand Canyon is in Pennsylvania? Well, maybe not the MAIN Grand Canyon, but Pennsylvania has its own! Another name for it is Pine Creek Gorge or the "Crown Jewel of Pennsylvania."

The gorge is 47 miles long and about 1,000 feet deep. The canyon was carved during the Ice Age by water that overflowed the banks of a glacial lake and ate away the soft rock bit by bit.

When we got out of the car, Josh showed me how to strap on cross-country skis. The woods were so quiet. All we could hear was the snow crunching and our huffing breath. Then we heard branches snapping. A whole bunch of deer bounded across the trail in front of us! Their white tails bobbed up and down as they ran. I wanted to move as fast as they did, but I shuffled more like an awkward duck on those skis.

Willy had a great idea. When he wasn't snuggled inside my jacket, he hopped down to the ground and made snow designs with his wings. Josh and I joined him and made snow angels. Aunt Fay worried that we'd get cold, and we did (a little). But luckily Uncle Richard brought along a thermos of hot chocolate, which warmed us right up. Yum!

Love from your snow angel,
Abby

On the tenth day of Christmas, my cousin gave to me . . .

10 deer a-leaping

9 sailors swabbing, **8** birds a-singing,
7 spooky spirits, **6** bumping buggies, **5** golden stars,
4 ringing rocks, **3** milk cows, **2** whoopie pies,
and a partridge in a hemlock tree.

Dear Mom and Dad,

Today we drove to Williamsport where the Little League Baseball World Series is played. The games have been held every August since 1947. I could feel the excitement as Josh and Uncle Richard described the game, and I could almost imagine players on the field and the crack of the bat. Maybe we can come next August and watch? We could eat popcorn and do the seventh-inning stretch—except there are only six innings in Little League! Fooled you! Back in the car, Aunt Fay sang "Take Me Out to the Ball Game" and Willy kept time by flapping his wings.

Then we hit the slopes in the Poconos. This time I didn't have to worry about having long skis strapped to my feet. We went tubing!

The Pocono Mountains have a 200-foot vertical drop. Some of the tubing chutes are 1,000 feet long. We jumped on special inner tubes and hung on for one very wild ride! Willy sat on the tube with me. He squawked when we hit a bump and went flying! Don't worry—he caught up with us at the bottom of the hill.

Love,
Abby

On the eleventh day of Christmas, my cousin gave to me . . .

11 tubes a-zooming

10 deer a-leaping, 9 sailors swabbing, 8 birds a-singing,
7 spooky spirits, 6 bumping buggies, 5 golden stars, 4 ringing rocks,
3 milk cows, 2 whoopie pies, and a partridge in a hemlock tree.

Dear Mom and Dad,

We're back in Philadelphia for my last day of vacation and a very special musical event. Uncle Richard is one of the bell ringers at Saint Mark's Church. Aunt Fay says that ringing is a huge team effort and a lot harder than it looks. The tenor bell weighs over 2,000 pounds, so it takes a lot of coordination and skill to pull the rope and make it ring at just the right moment in a song. Everyone has to work together.

The smaller bells have a higher pitch; the larger ones a deeper sound. Each one is attached to a rope that has a brightly colored "sally"—that's colored wool woven into the rope so you know exactly where to grab it. Ringers swing the bell through a full arc to make it sing. What an amazing sound!

Afterward, we took handbells and walked to Rittenhouse Square, one of the original five parks planned for the city by William Penn way back in 1681. At first, it was called "Southwest Square." It was renamed in 1825 in honor of David Rittenhouse, a leading 18th-century scientist, Philadelphian, and patriot.

At the park, we put on a bell concert of our own. Then Willy strutted through the park and led us in a big parade!

I already miss Pennsylvania, but I can't wait to show you all the gifts Josh gave me. Maybe you could rent a really big truck to pick me up at the airport?

Your almost-home daughter,
Abby

On the twelfth day of Christmas,
my cousin gave to me . . .

12 handbell ringers

11 tubes a-zooming, **10** deer a-leaping, **9** sailors swabbing,
8 birds a-singing, **7** spooky spirits, **6** bumping buggies,
5 golden stars, **4** ringing rocks, **3** milk cows, **2** whoopie pies,
and a partridge in a hemlock tree.

Pennsylvania: The Keystone State

State Capital: Harrisburg • **Largest City**: Philadelphia • **State Abbreviation**: PA • **State Bird**: the ruffed grouse • **State Flower**: the mountain laurel • **State Tree**: the eastern hemlock • **State Insect**: the firefly • **State Fossil**: the trilobite (*Phacops rana*) • **State Animal**: the white-tailed deer • **State Fish**: the brook trout • **State Dog**: the Great Dane • **State Beverage**: milk • **State Ship**: the US Brig *Niagara* • **State Motto**: "Virtue, Liberty, and Independence" • **State Song**: "Pennsylvania," lyrics and music by Eddie Khoury and Ronnie Bonner

Some Famous Pennsylvanians:

Louisa May Alcott (1832–1888) was born in Germantown. Writing was an early passion. She wrote *Hospital Sketches* (1863) based on her work as a Civil War nurse and, most famously, *Little Women* (1868), based on experiences with her sisters.

Daniel Boone (1734–1820), born on the edge of the Pennsylvania wilderness, was a frontiersman, explorer, soldier, and judge, and described as the "greatest woodsman" in US history. At the Daniel Boone Homestead historical site in Birdsboro you can visit the restored log cabin where Boone was born and raised.

James Buchanan (1791–1868) was the fifteenth president of the United States. So far he is the only president from Pennsylvania and the only bachelor president. He not only was born in Pennsylvania (Cove Gap), but he was educated there, too (attended Dickinson College). He died in Lancaster.

Stephen Foster (1826–1864), known as the first great American songwriter, was born in Lawrenceville, east of Pittsburgh. A self-taught musician and composer, he was inspired by popular folk music. Stephen Foster wrote hundreds of songs, many still popular today. They include "Oh! Susanna!" and "Swanee River."

Martha Graham (1894–1991) was a modern dancer and choreographer born just outside of Pittsburgh. The Martha Graham Dance Company, which she founded, is the oldest modern dance company in America. She has been described as "the mother of modern dance" and was the first dancer to perform at the White House.

Gene Kelly (1912–1996) was born in Pittsburgh and educated at Pennsylvania State College and the University of Pittsburgh. He was an actor, dancer, and choreographer whose athletic style of movement and playful ballet technique added new excitement to film. He had the lead role in *Singin' in the Rain* (1952).

Margaret Mead (1901–1978), born in Philadelphia, was a famous writer and cultural anthropologist, a scientist who studies the development of human cultures. Margaret Mead wrote bestselling books about the lives of children in different places around the world and helped pioneer the use of pictures in anthropology.

To my parents, Margaret and David, who showed me from an early age that learning can be fun! And to my children, David and Dayna, who keep me young at heart. —M.P.L.

To my family and friends, who have always dreamed even bigger for me than I have for myself. —R.D.

STERLING CHILDREN'S BOOKS
New York

An Imprint of Sterling Publishing
387 Park Avenue South
New York, NY 10016

STERLING CHILDREN'S BOOKS and the distinctive Sterling Children's Books logo are trademarks of Sterling Publishing Co., Inc.

Text © 2014 by Martha Peaslee Levine
Illustrations © 2014 by Rachel Dougherty
The original illustrations for this book were created with acrylic paint.
Designed by Andrea Miller

HERSHEY'S KISSES® Brand Chocolates is a registered trademark of The Hershey Company, Hershey, PA 17033-0815. All rights reserved.

ISBN 978-1-4549-0889-0

Library of Congress Cataloging-in-Publication Data

Levine, Martha Peaslee.
  The twelve days of Christmas in Pennsylvania / by Martha Peaslee Levine ; illustrated by Rachel Dougherty.
    pages cm
  Summary: Abby writes a letter home each of the twelve days she spends exploring Pennsylvania at Christmastime, as her cousin Josh shows her everything from a partridge in a hemlock tree to twelve handbell ringers. Includes facts about Pennsylvania.
  ISBN 978-1-4549-0889-0
  [1. Pennsylvania--Fiction. 2. Christmas--Fiction. 3. Cousins--Fiction. 4. Letters--Fiction.] I. Dougherty, Rachel, 1988- illustrator. II. Title.
  PZ7.L57846Tw 2014
  [E]--dc23
                    2013042062

Distributed in Canada by Sterling Publishing
^{c}/o Canadian Manda Group, 165 Dufferin Street
Toronto, Ontario, Canada M6K 3H6
Distributed in the United Kingdom by GMC Distribution Services
Castle Place, 166 High Street, Lewes, East Sussex, England BN7 1XU
Distributed in Australia by Capricorn Link (Australia) Pty. Ltd.
P.O. Box 704, Windsor, NSW 2756, Australia

For information about custom editions, special sales, and premium and corporate purchases,
please contact Sterling Special Sales at 800-805-5489 or specialsales@sterlingpublishing.com.

Manufactured in China
Lot #:
2 4 6 8 10 9 7 5 3 1
07/14

www.sterlingpublishing.com/kids